# SANTA CLAUS

*The*

# WORLD'S NUMBER ONE TOY EXPERT

# SANTA CLAUS
## *The*
# WORLD'S NUMBER ONE TOY EXPERT

Marla Frazee

**SCHOLASTIC INC.**

New York   Toronto   London   Auckland   Sydney
Mexico City   New Delhi   Hong Kong   Buenos Aires

For Allyn, one of the elves

ISBN 0-439-90087-5

12 11 10 9 8 7 6 5 4 3 2 1          6 7 8 9 10 11/0

Printed in the U.S.A.                    08

First Scholastic printing, September 2006

The illustrations in this book were done in black pencil and gouache on Strathmore paper, hot press finish.
The display and text lettering were created by Marla Frazee.

No one knows more about kids
than Santa Claus.
He is the world's
number one
kid
expert.

He meets a lot of kids.
He listens to them.
He visits with the brave ones who hop
right up on his lap.

He watches the
shy ones
who
don't.

And he even has his own Santa Claus ways of getting to know kids who never have a chance to meet him in person.

He takes lots and lots of notes,

compiles all his research,

and works
   long, long hours
      the whole year round.

Nothing makes him happier.

No one knows
more about toys
than Santa Claus.

He is the world's number one toy expert.

He finds the best toys in the whole world.

He makes sure they are fun to play with.

He checks them out to see if they are sturdy.

Or not.

He even has his own
Santa Claus ways
of making the
cozy toys
become
EXTRA
special.

He carefully inspects each toy,

makes the final selections,

and works
long, long hours
the whole year
round.

He loves his job.

No one knows more about gifts than Santa Claus.

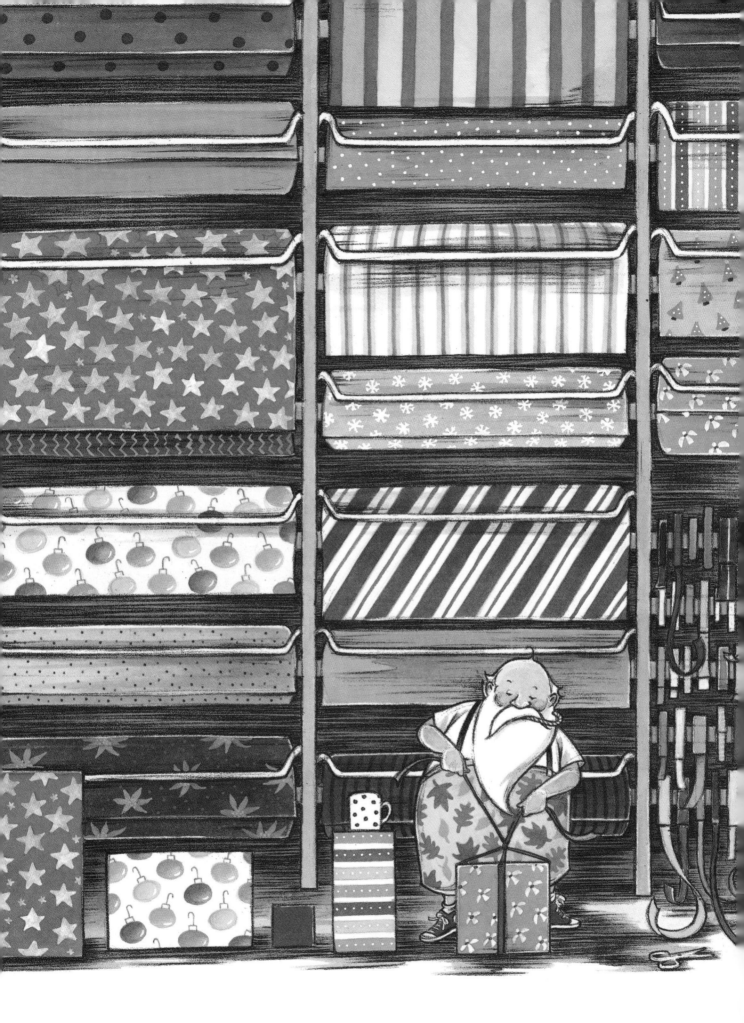

He is the world's number one gift expert.

When
  it is
    almost
      Christmas,
Santa thinks very hard about all the kids he knows so well.

He thinks very hard about all the toys he's played with.

He works carefully
to match up
each particular toy
with each
particular
kid.

He changes
his mind
many times, and...

after hours and hours of very hard work, he gets it all figured out.

And then
on Christmas morning,
Santa Claus gives the
exact right toy
to the
exact right
kid,

99.9 % of the time.

That's almost always!

(Well, no one is
perfect.
Not even
Santa
Claus.)

Then when the day is over
and all his work is finished,
Santa Claus goes home and unwraps
the special gift
he picked out
for
himself.

And it's almost always just exactly what he wanted.